D0624068

Francine Francine the Beach Party Queen!

written & illustrated by

Audrey Colman

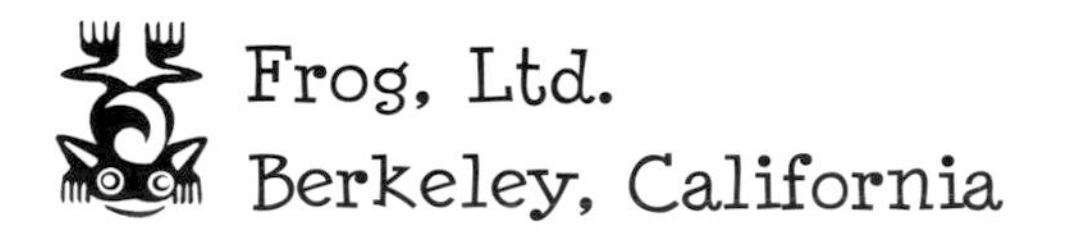

Frog, Ltd.
Berkeley, California

For for my niece and nephew, Sarah and Zohar,
whose features are hidden inside these pages
and within various characters in the story.

Thanks, Dad, for providing me with some great lines,
and to both my parents, Marcia and Oscar Colman,
for the entertaining brainstorming sessions.

For information contact Frog, Ltd. c/o North Atlantic Books.

Published by Frog, Ltd.

Frog, Ltd. books are distributed by North Atlantic Books,
P.O. Box 12327, Berkeley, California 94712

ISBN 1-58394-074-X

Library of Congress Catalog Card Number 2003001717

Book design by Audrey Colman and Paula Morrison

Printed in Singapore

1 2 3 4 5 6 7 8 9 / 09 08 07 06 05 04 03

The Crabapples said that I look kind of dumb.
So I have a big head and a small skinny bum.
Big deal! Every animal has their own style.
In our own way, each of us is worthwhile.

They gave me a perfectly fine place to sleep,
two walks every day, and a bath every week.

But I was still lonely, my days oh so bland,
with the boring, persnickety Crabapple clan.

They all acted serious, but I felt delirious,
so filled up with fire that I never tired.

Sure, I had antics that caused them to groan,
but I also had some complaints of my own.

Bland
Brand
Nuggets
francine
Tofooti
Frooti

Every day I got fed the same boring food—
I could never try theirs. Wasn't that rude?
I dreamt every night about tasting new treats.
I longed to try veggies, or maybe some sweets!

Sometimes they acted as though I weren't there.
They'd chat right above me. 'Twas quite hard to bear.
I'd wag my tail wildly, look from face to face,
but they just ignored me. I felt so out of place.

I'd be so happy before every walk,
    but then I was punished for stopping to talk
    with a dog or a cat friend, or even a bird.
They just yanked me along. It was truly absurd!
If a fresh pile of dog poo got me excited,
    they never noticed that I was delighted.
They dragged me right past it! Why couldn't they see
    that a lot of the best things around us are free?

Candy the ten-year-old often got cross,

and even the toddler thought he was my boss!

I know I act silly, but I wasn't bad.

Whenever I played the whole family got mad.

Sometimes Mr. Crabapple, and Mrs. as well,

or all the Crabapples together would yell,

"You're driving us crazy, you're right underfoot.

We should just buy a toy dog. At least they stay put!"

There was only so much that a lady could take.
I finally decided 'twas time for a break.
Straight out of the window I jumped in a flash
without my umbrella or even some cash.
If I had to, I'd travel to Paris or Prague.
I just wanted the freedom to act like a dog!

I dashed to the park where the dogs go to play
and had such a good time I decided to stay!

But later my new friends all headed for home.
The mood sure felt different when I was alone.

The darkness grew darker, winds started to howl,

and I felt so afraid I decided to growl

at nothing specific, just into the air ...

I wanted to scare off whatever was there.

Then I got hungry, but mostly just tired,

so I searched all around, found a spot, and retired.

The Dancing Fools
studio

I woke in the morning curled up on the step

of the friendliest dance troupe that one could expect.

They called themselves Dancing Fools, but they were NOT—

they were all really smart, and they laughed quite a lot.

They traipsed through the door with me right behind.

I was truly accepted as one of their kind!

Munching popcorn and cookies and sipping green tea,

I could hardly believe they were sharing with me!

There was singing and dancing and laughing at jokes

and hugging and cuddling and snuggling with folks.

The head dancer called out, "You make us all laugh,

Francine, please stay with us and join our great staff!

Your barking is fine 'cause we all talk a lot."

My old rules of silence could then be forgot.

I was so excited, I never would leave.

They certainly loved me, 'twas hard to believe!

I could act really goofy. They didn't care.
My character charmed them. I guess I have flair!

The wildest dance steps were my very own,

and soon they all followed me. I set the tone!

“Let’s go to the beach,” we all cried as if one,
“to frolic and splash around, just have some fun—

right out in the open. The whole town will see
how easy it is to be happy and free!"

I finally can just be myself for a change
without getting punished for acting so "strange."
That's all I can ask for, to not be left out,
and that's what my whole crazy story's about!